© 2008 Dami International srl, Milano-Firenze

This 2009 edition published by Sandy Creek
by arrangement with Dami International srl.

Sandy Creek
122 Fifth Avenue
New York, N.Y. 10011

ISBN - 13:   978 - 1 - 4351 - 1157 - 8

Printed and bound in China

1   3   5   7   9   10   8   6   4   2

from an idea by ANDREA DAMI

Illustrations by Marco Campanella
Text by Anna Casalis
Design by Stefania Pavin

TIP THE MOUSE

DOESN'T WANT TO EAT

Illustrated by

Marco Campanella

SANDY CREEK

"So much snow! Brrr … it's cold outside! Teddy, we're lucky to be here at home, in our warm and cozy room!"

"Tip, run and wash your paws. Dinner's ready!" Tip's mother calls out.

TIIIP!!

"Oh, eating is so boring!" Tip says, crossing his arms in protest. His voice starts to tremble, which can only mean one thing – a big tantrum is on its way!

"Come on, Tip, eat your carrot soup! It's always been your favorite, and I went out of my way to pick the sweetest baby carrots in the garden!"

"I don't like carrots any more! They're a funny color!"

Tip the Mouse doesn't want to hear about the soup. He even refuses to eat his favorite cheese.

"I don't like cheese either! I just want some candy!" And with this, Tip gets down and goes to his room, taking Teddy with him.

Mom is quite angry now. "Candy? You have to eat all your soup if you want to become a strong and handsome mouse like your father. You should consider yourself lucky to have a nice warm meal. The animals in the woods, with all this cold and snow, can't find anything to eat at all!"

Hmphh!

Tip...

Tip the Mouse doesn't want to show it, but his mom's words make him sad – he loves his friends in the woods.

"Knock! Knock!" Who can it be?

"It's me, Cicada! Open up, please! It's freezing out here!" Even though she's wearing a wool scarf and a cap, Cicada looks frozen right down to her bones.

"Could you spare a spoonful of hot soup, or a piece of cheese-rind?" Cicada asks in a tiny voice.

"It's the same story every winter, isn't it?" says Mom. "You didn't remember to put anything aside over the summer! Instead of stocking up, you sang and danced. Now it's winter and you're starving and cold."

Mom's not really angry though – she just worries about poor Cicada.

"Come in. I'll give you the dinner I cooked for this silly little mouse who doesn't want to eat anything but candy!"

The carrot soup is still steaming. Cicada, without waiting to be asked twice, grabs the plate. She gobbles down the soup, one big spoonful after another.

"This is wonderful! My compliments to the chef!"

When she has finished eating, Cicada says to Tip, "Why didn't you want to eat your dinner? You have no idea what it means to be hungry and to have nothing else to eat but some dry pinecones and a few pieces of frozen bark!"

Before leaving, Cicada sings a thank-you song to Tip and his mother.

Tip the Mouse thinks about what his friend has just told him.

"Dry pinecones and bark! How yucky! Umm … Mom, is there any food left?" Tip's appetite has suddenly come back.

"Of course, my darling little mouse! There are still some baby carrots and cheese." Luckily, his mother had cooked a large dinner.

Tip the Mouse empties his plate and happily licks his whiskers. Mom sees that her little one has learned a lesson today.

"Mom, I won't be silly anymore. When it's time to eat my dinner, I'll think of poor Cicada and the other animals in the woods… "